Animal Friends

Giant Coloring & Activity Book

Modern Publishing
A Division of Unisystems, Inc.
New York, New York 10022
Printed in the U.S.A.

Zebras

Kittens

Bunny

START

END

SEE ANSWERS

LOST LION
This baby lion is trying to make his way back home! See if you can help him by following the correct path through the maze!

Ladybugs

Sea Lion

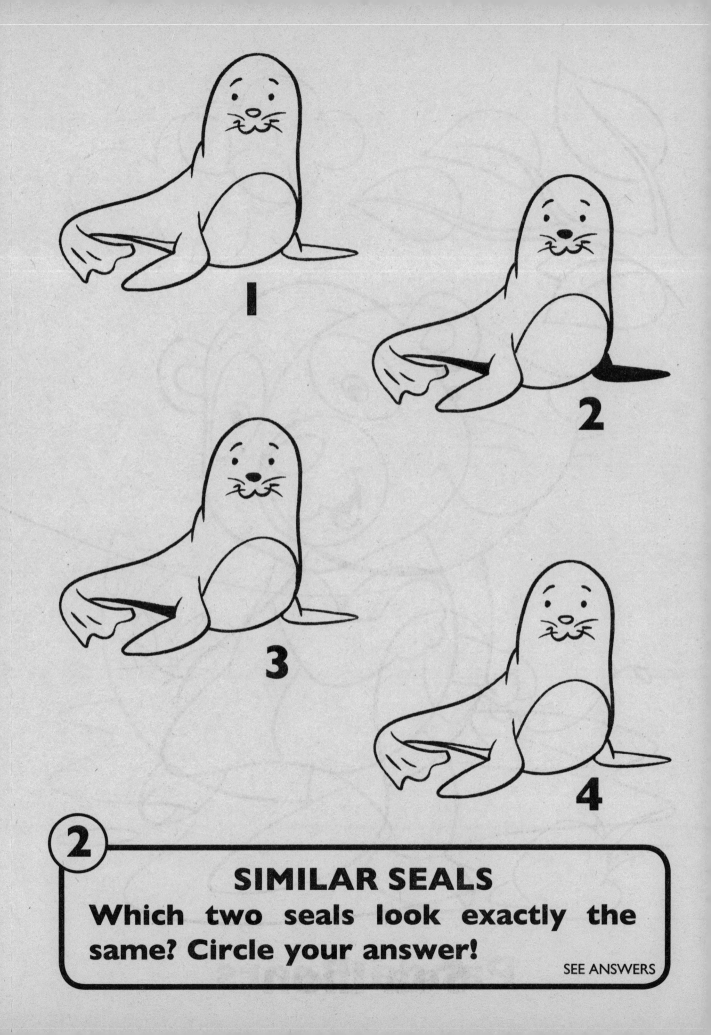

1

2

3

4

SEE ANSWERS

2

SIMILAR SEALS
Which two seals look exactly the same? Circle your answer!

Panda Bears

Kangaroos

Lobster

3 **HOW MANY BUBBLES?**
How many bubbles do you see coming out of the baby fish's mouth? Write your answer on the line!

_____

SEE ANSWERS

FRIENDLY FOX
How many words can you make using the letters in the words FRIENDLY FOX?

_____ _____

_____ _____

_____ _____

_____ _____

SEE ANSWERS

Hippopotamus

Turtles

Aardvark

1

2

3

4

SEE ANSWERS

5

EGG-CELLENT EGGS
Which nest has the most eggs in it?
Circle your answer.

Piglets

Ponies

Hamster

6

COOL KOALA

Unscramble the letters to reveal the name of the continent where most Koala Bears are found!

A T R L A S I U A

- - - - - - - - -

SEE ANSWERS

Flamingos

Seahorses

7

CHIPMUNK MUNCHIES

Chipmunks like to eat lots of nuts and berries! What do you think this chipmunk is having for dinner today? Draw some ideas in the space below!

Snail

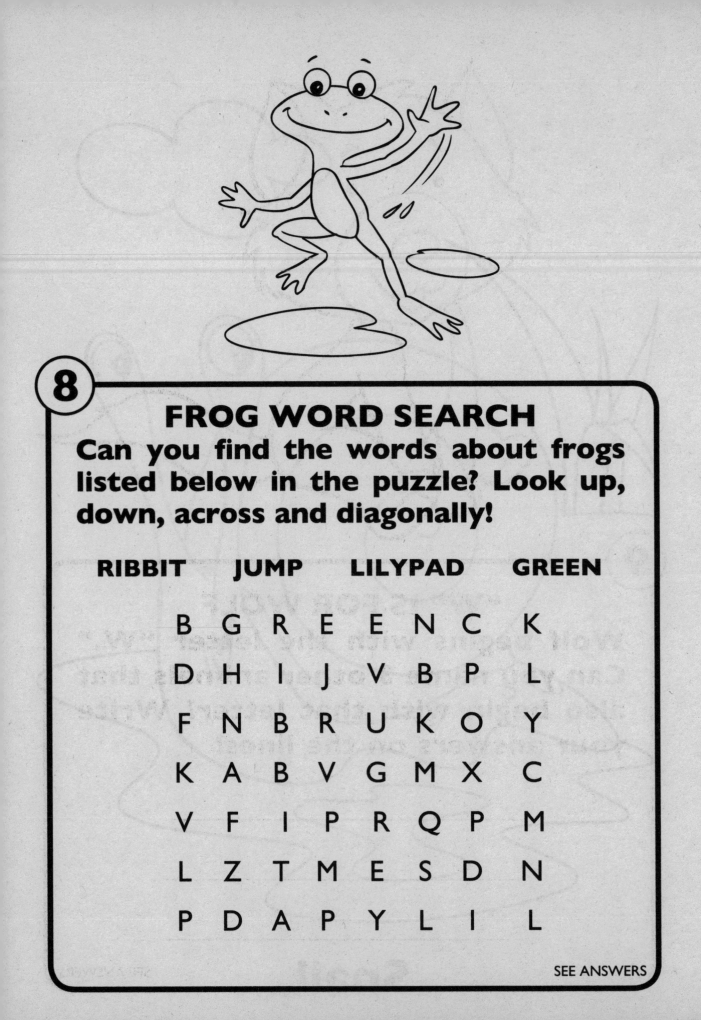

FROG WORD SEARCH

Can you find the words about frogs listed below in the puzzle? Look up, down, across and diagonally!

RIBBIT JUMP LILYPAD GREEN

```
B G R E E N C K
D H I J V B P L
F N B R U K O Y
K A B V G M X C
V F I P R Q P M
L Z T M E S D N
P D A P Y L I L
```

SEE ANSWERS

9

"W" IS FOR WOLF

Wolf begins with the letter "W." Can you name 3 other animals that also begin with that letter? Write your answers on the lines!

_____

_____

_____

SEE ANSWERS

Dolphins

Butterflies

10

COOL CODE

Using the code, write the letters on the line to find out what the cheetah is known for!

1=A   2=B   3=C   4=D   5=E   6=F

7=G   8=H   9=I   10=J   11=K   12=L

13=M   14=N   15=O   16=P   17=Q   18=R

19=S   20=T   21=U   22=V   23=W   24=X

25=Y   26=Z

___ ___ ___ ___ ___ ___ ___
6   1   19   20   5   19   20

___ ___ ___ ___
12   1   14   4

___ ___ ___ ___ ___ ___ !
1   14   9   13   1   12

SEE ANSWERS

Calf

Walruses

11

RHYME TIME

How many words can you think of that rhyme with BEE? See if you can name 5 in under 1 minute! Go!

_____

_____

_____

_____

_____

SEE ANSWERS

PUPPY PATH

Help this puppy get to his dog bowl by following the correct path through the maze!

SEE ANSWERS

Gorilla

Grasshopper

13

MISSING LETTERS

Fill in the missing vowels (A, E, I, O or U) to spell the name of this large animal!

_ L _ P H _ NT

SEE ANSWERS

Eagle

Frogs

Skunks

(14)

KITTEN JOKE

Write the letter that comes AFTER each letter given to determine the answer to the joke!

What is a cat's favorite color?

_ _ _ _ _ _ _ _ _ _ _

O   T   Q   Q   Q   Q   O   K   D

SEE ANSWERS

Stingray

Giraffes

15

LOOK AT THE LLAMAS
Which baby llama looks different than the others? Circle your answer!

SEE ANSWERS

Lamb

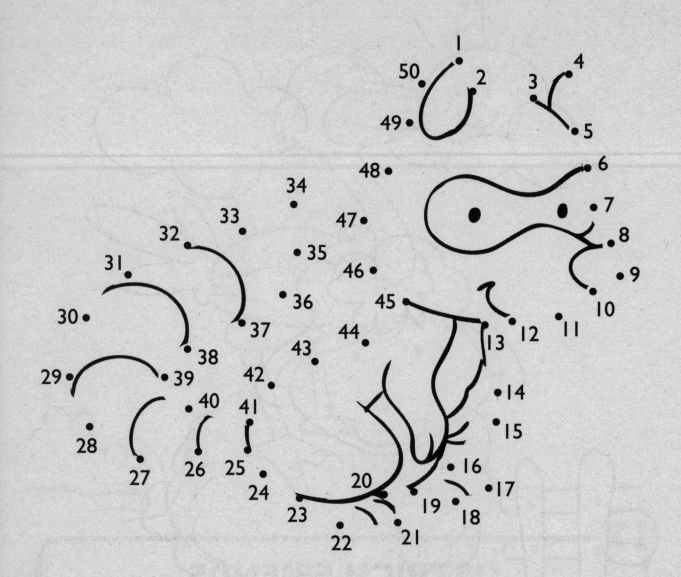

SEE ANSWERS

16

DOT-TO-DOT
Connect the dots from 1 to 50 to see the baby raccoon!

17

OSTRICH FRIENDS

An ostrich is a type of bird. Can you name 3 other types of birds? Write your answers on the lines!

_____

_____

_____ SEE ANSWERS

Deer

Polar Bears

1

2

3

4

18

INSECT INSPECTION
Which of the animals is **NOT** an insect? Circle your answer!

SEE ANSWERS

19

HAPPY HIPPO

A hippo has _____ legs.

A hippo has _____ ears.

A hippo has _____ tail.

SEE ANSWERS

umble Be s

Turkeys

Caterpillar

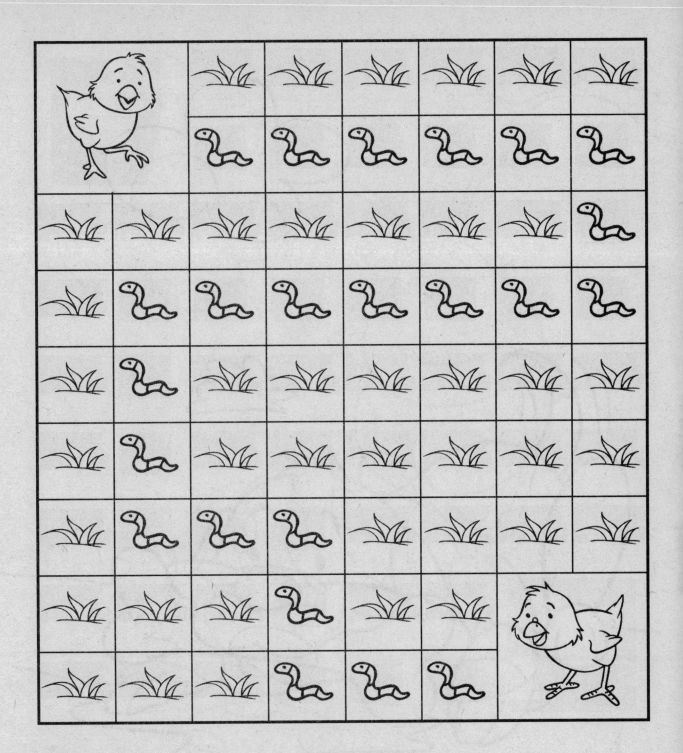

SEE ANSWERS

20

THE WORM WAY

Help this baby chick get to his friend
by following the correct path, which
is made up of only worms!

Puppies

Snake

G R A S O P C Y G T Y P C O S A R G F E V C

SEE ANSWERS

21

AROUND THE WHEEL

To reveal the name of this baby animal, start at the arrow and write down every **THIRD** letter in order on the lines!

_____ _____ _____ _____ _____ _____ _____

Sharks

Ostrich

22

COOL CODE

Using the code, write the letters on the line to find out what a porcupine's body is covered with!

1=A	2=B	3=C	4=D	5=E	6=F
7=G	8=H	9=I	10=J	11=K	12=L
13=M	14=N	15=O	16=P	17=Q	18=R
19=S	20=T	21=U	22=V	23=W	24=X
25=Y	26=Z				

___ ___ ___ ___ ___ ___
17   21   9   12   12   19

SEE ANSWERS

rhinoceros**_s**

Jellyfish

 = ___

 = ___

 = ___

 = ___

23 MONKEY MATH
Add the number of monkeys together!

SEE ANSWERS

Camels

24

HOW MANY LAMBS?
How many lambs do you see on the page? Write your answer on the line!

_____

SEE ANSWERS

ANSWERS

#1 LOST LION

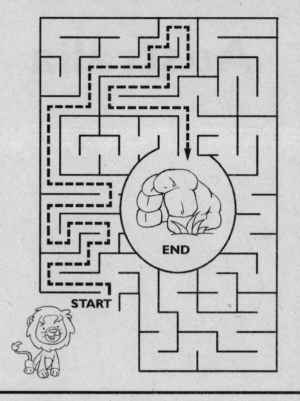

START

END

#2 SIMILAR SEALS

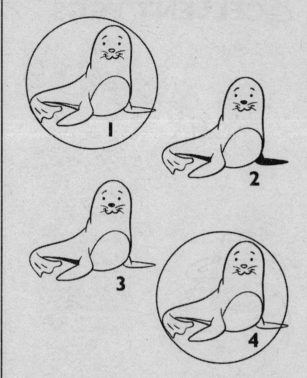

1

2

3

4

#3
HOW MANY BUBBLES?

8

#4 FRIENDLY FOX
Some possible answers are:

Fry, Rod, Den, Fly, Lend, Lie, Role, For

ANSWERS

#5 EGG-CELLENT EGGS

1   2

3   4

#6 COOL KOALA

Australia

#8 FROG WORD SEARCH

#9 "W" IS FOR WOLF

Some possible answers are:

Whale
Walrus
Woodpecker

ANSWERS

#10 COOL CODE

**Fastest
Land
Animal**

#11 RHYME TIME

Some possible
answers are:

**See, Tea,
Me, Tree,
Knee**

#12 PUPPY PATH

#13 MISSING LETTERS

Elephant

ANSWERS

#14 KITTEN JOKE

Purrrrple

#15 LOOK AT THE LLAMAS

#16 DOT-TO-DOT

#17 OSTRICH FRIENDS

Some possible answers are:

Eagle
Robin
Dove
Seagull
Blue Jay

ANSWERS

#18 INSECT INSPECTION

#19 HAPPY HIPPO

A hippo has <u>4</u> legs.

A hippo has <u>2</u> ears.

A hippo has <u>1</u> tail.

#20 THE WORM WAY

#21 AROUND THE WHEEL

Otter

ANSWERS

#22 COOL CODE

Quills

#23 MONKEY MATH

$2 + 3 = 5$
$3 + 4 = 7$
$2 + 2 = 4$
$5 + 1 = 6$

#24 HOW MANY LAMBS?

11